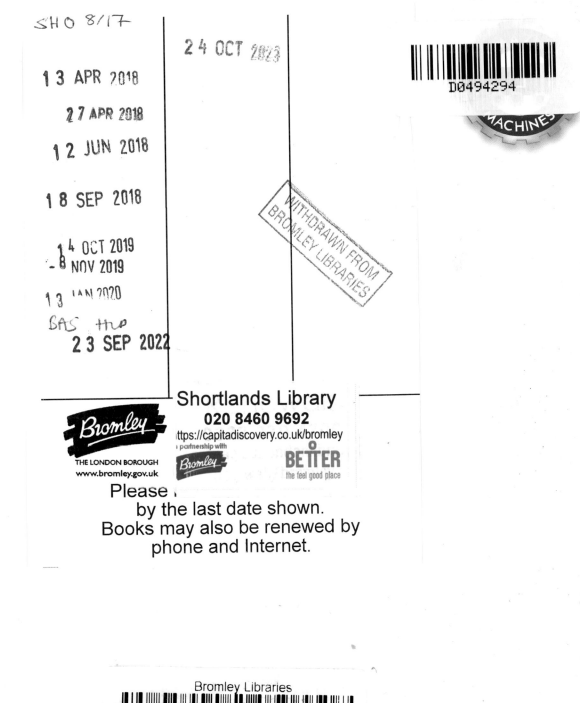

## Shortlands Library
### 020 8460 9692
https://capitadiscovery.co.uk/bromley
in partnership with

*Bromley*

THE LONDON BOROUGH
www.bromley.gov.uk

*Bromley*

BETTER
the feel good place

Please
by the last date shown.
Books may also be renewed by
phone and Internet.

*For Arlo Harold Douglas Cope – T.M.*
*For Betsy – A.P.*

KINGFISHER

First published 2017 by Kingfisher,
an imprint of Macmillan Children's Books
20 New Wharf Road, London N1 9RR

ISBN 978-0-7534-3997-5

Text copyright © Tony Mitton 2016
Illustrations copyright © Ant Parker 2016
Designed by Anthony Hannant (LittleRedAnt) 2016

A CIP catalogue record for this book is available
from the British Library

Printed in China
9 8 7 6 5 4 3 2 1
1TR/1216/HH/UG/128MA

# MARVELLUUS
# MOTORBIKES

Tony Mitton
and
Ant Parker

KINGFISHER

Motorbikes are marvellous.
They growl as they go past.

They're sharp and sleek and snazzy.
They're flashy and they're fast.

The motorbikes of long ago
seemed such a crazy scheme.

They rattled and they chugged along
with engines run on steam.

But motorbikes today are powerful.
Look at this machine –

it's built for easy cruising.
It's classy and it's clean.

When you mount a motorbike,
you use both hands to steer.
Your right foot works the back brake.
Your left's for changing gear.

Your left hand works the horn
and indicator, when there's need.
Your right hand twists the throttle
to give you extra speed.

If you only want to ride
across your town or city,
a scooter may be suitable.
It's simple, light and pretty.

But if you go long distances,
here's something you might like –
with windscreen and more storage
it's a proper touring bike.

Here's a zippy fire-bike,
for fires in tricky places.
A motorbike can get to them
by squeezing through tight spaces.

And here's a medic's motorbike,
so speedy and so neat,
it slips through heavy traffic
on a busy city street.

A sport bike is a motorbike
built to speed and race.

To ride a bike like this
you really need to be an Ace.

Dirt bikes are much lighter
but they're rugged and they're tough.

They snarl through mud or sand or ice,
on rocky ground or rough.

Stunt riders use their motorbikes
for turning in the air!

You'd need to practise very hard
before you'd even dare...

A sidecar with a motorbike
easily takes three.

We're off to have a picnic
at the seaside now – whoopee!

# Motorbike parts

**accelerator**
this controls the flow of petrol through the engine and the speed of the motorbike

**headlight**
this helps the rider to see and be seen in the dark - it lights up the road ahead

**petrol tank**
this contains the petrol that the engine needs to make it run

**mudguards**
these shield the motorbike and rider from mud, water and grit that are thrown up by the wheels

**exhaust pipe**
this lets out the waste gases from the engine as the petrol is burned

**brakes**
the discs at the centre of each wheel can press down to make the motorbike stop